ESSAY ON AIR

Books by Reg Saner

Essay On Air
So This Is The Map
Climbing Into The Roots

ESSAY ON AIR

REG SANER

AN OHIO REVIEW BOOK
Athens, Ohio

The author wishes to thank the University of Colorado's
Council on Research and Creative Work,
the National Endowment for the Arts, and the
Creede Repertory Theatre of Creede, Colorado
for their generous support.

Cover design by Jack Keely.
Set in 11 point Garamond by Sans Serif and
printed by C J Krehbiel Co, Cincinnati, Ohio.

Publication of this book has been aided
by a grant from the Ohio Arts Council.

Library of Congress Cataloging in Publication Data
Saner, Reg.
  Essay On Air.

  (Ohio Review Books)
  I. Title.
PS3569.A5254E8   1984   811'.54   84-2229
ISBN 0-942148-03-7
ISBN 0-942148-02-9 (pbk)

Acknowledgments

Some of the poems in this collection appeared originally in the following publications:

Aloe
    If You've A Leaning Toward Pillars Of Fire

Atlantic
    Green Feathers

Crazy Horse
    At Luxon; Late Roman Mosaic: Husband And Wife

Cream City Review
    Poem (Less and less. . . .); The Blue Changes; Wearing Breakfast For Two

The Georgia Review
    Rimlight And Pupil

New Boston Review
    Mountain Lake: Gore Range

New Mexico Humanities Review
    Cigar

THE OHIO REVIEW
    Vespers; The Vesuvius Variations; Where The Desert Knows One Or Two Words

Pacific Poetry And Fiction Review
    Essay On Air

The Paris Review
    The Fifth Season; Road Life

Pendragon
    When My Name's A Camper's Spoon; The Sleeping Porch

Poetry
    The Man-In-The-Moon; Eastward From Somewhere: San Vitale, Ravenna; In The
        Iron Trough Of The Year; Neither Lions Ravens Nor White Toads; Ghiberti's
        Baptistery Doors Revisited

Poetry Northwest
    Why I Marvel At Certain Noises

Poetry Now
    Skiing Alone Near The Divide; Tiber (as *In Italiam*); Ed And Me

Prairie Schooner
    Aspen Oktoberfest; Jane; The Fire Thief; North; West; Anne, Your Name's Mouth And Kiss;
        Song For Sisyphus

Slow Loris
    Where The Desert Knows One Or Two Words

Southern Poetry Review
    Prospectus

Telescope
    Equinox

Three Rivers Poetry Journal
    The Tongue As Red Dog

Writers' Forum
    Out Of The Ashes Of Last Summer's Green Cigar

For my father
Reginald Anthony Saner
too late

Contents

The Tongue as Red Dog

When "soul" was still locked landscape
frankly empty as steppes, a few maimed weeds
tried standing up for lyres
the wind strummed. But that wasn't it.

To the east, broods of heliotrope pigeons
meant to be "daybreak"
or "sunset" and couldn't tell which. Everything
that had swum up through the mire
wanted to speak.

Occasionally the vast stands of blue timber
launched a hurtle and dart of feathered flutes
coming close, yet not quite "utterance"—
more "reservoir." Whose ripples, like concentric syllables,
went on dying toward "shore."

Thus epochs.

And the nights wore mere sandpaper
mistaken, glittering like "stars," gnawing rough edges.

Who could say? A voice might yet turn up
if only a blur, one common as lichen
grown brighter than ice. When lo! Over the dumb rim
of the spectrum, out of some animal idiom
for water circled with daylight
tripped this nimble little red dog
leading an odd constellation of bones.

Feeling out
new ways for them, drawing them further
into the astonishing grammar of fire,
into earthy declensions of air,
into the green syntax of rain.

ONE

Where the Desert Knows One or Two Words

Hours south
out of the walls, trunks, red pedestals of Monument Valley
a desert still levels to meet us
as light
knowing one or two words.

And still the Arizona plateau miles after sundown.

So we pitch the blue tent by heart
knowing we'll sleep outside it. I ransack for tomatoes
one-handed, and onion, sipping beer spiked with ice
you seine up from the cooler.

As always we find ourselves breaking trances
entered just by stopping to listen,
where each word, least motion
sets off our hush. You say, "Know how hamburger sizzles?"

"Pebbles, crunching past under Jeep tires."

And we talk late
mostly in pauses thinner than whisper,
looking far into night's firesteps
even asleep, two faces
offering their pale, upturned blur
where the meteors keep coming to die.

Mountain Lake: Gore Range

In an hour or two, and carefully,
a geologist will chip open a seam of fish.

Up from nowhere but ripples
trout blurt into light marrying them
like a second element
stolen, then disappear clean as knives
become leaves, toward the floor
of the lake.

In an hour or two, when the blue lake is clouds
and the clouds have gone black.

The Man-in-the-Moon

Like a slow walk
as the man-in-the-moon's perfect sadness
my father left this life unfinished, traveling west
gifted and lucky in nothing
but patience.

The fox den is pups, nipping, leaping Jimson tips
breasting dry tassels like dolphins
in snow. Nearby, a fur-bearing bone. Porcupine?
The single book he got through, or tried to—
what was it? Some travel thing
by Lowell Thomas. His opinions? Slow ones, almost none
in my hearing.

Animals aren't good at themselves
as we suppose, not always. Take left-footed dogs, deaf bats
presumably, horses self-foundered, antelopes charging
barbed wire at high speeds. These days my walks
take in more territory, taking less time
to be wise. What was it he wanted? Never a clue
or once maybe, drinking. His eyes behind glasses
oily and thick as his tongue, slurring
of all syllables a word I'd supposed not in his world
sounding like "poet."

The more I wade through the less I recall
reading much of him. Yet if that trudge to work
you despise and back home so as to have one
isn't a sort of a measure
what is?

High in a 100-foot elm
chainsawed when the house was leveled for cars
I once watched a grey squirrel timing its leap, then miss
entirely. Details like bifocals, a fat face stewed

in its sweat, register-tapes in folds on the table,
the tumbler of water darkened with bourbon—how they glue
to their moment. Roads branching into
and out of a town arrived at
or not, following bloodlines, conjectures.

As he drank I drew back, impressed
with my future in deep centerfield, later, could be,
even in nightclubs.

Some cats've been nursed by dachshunds. We have one.
How many books do I own? By now more than I know,
shelves of blind owls. Few teachers, even,
use "vixen" with accuracy. The she-fox
tricks me away from her den, or hopes to, set off
by a haze of withered sedge, furze, buffalo grass,
holding poses
too visibly. A character actor whose role
is letting her future use her as bait.

These days I often consider how perfectly beaten
the moon must feel—where each loss
or terrible scar that could happen
has happened. Ears cocked she looks back at me
putting her red pelt on the line
daily as work. Did I scorn him on his own money?
Not really. Not always.

When what might've happened has happened
or not, leaving you more or less deeply impressive
as no one, the closer you draw
to allowing even the animals their share
explaining details of the story. This one you're writing
to leave to the loneliest part of the sky
for the man-in-the-moon to lip read and ignore
walking slowly forever.

Eastward From Somewhere:
San Vitale, Ravenna

A few shovelfuls of gravel
brilliantly thrown together and a stone dove
this clear paraclete
flies through gold rain.

At the top of the sky topping the vault
a severed hand wearing purple thread
stitches heaven to earth.
Robed in chipped rock, live coals,
glitters the court of Justinian, church and state,
while baffling as pond-light
the Empress Theodora's peplum mixes surface
with the depth of hammered dream
more weightless than anything we can remember.

It was an Empire.
It was an Earthly Paradise including these figures.

Two pebbly doves perch an urn. Their bills sip
at the Fountain of Life overflowing
basilica walls, past bushes of shattered glass.
Under mosaic antlers, stags that have been souls
lap from blue crinkles through forest so vast
and profound it hasn't a tree
recognizably ours.

Like her attendants Theodora smiles at the ease
with which we take color and line
for the intimate clarity, the utter within
of one perfectly gorgeous woman
no longer in motion.

It was an Empire.
It was this fire that pours through our fingers.
And eastward from somewhere, this tessera waterfall
voiceless.

21

Aspen Oktoberfest

Through an amber dazzle of aspen
the sun delves and paddles. The eye opens,
walks with that sun in its circles,
and closes.

Along the streambed I listen: crag chunks, pebbles, boulders
breasting torrent, whacking back at it, memorizing
the full past of a creek trailing from them like robes
as their fracture lines blunt and decide
on the strange, voluptuous forms of believers in water.

Trunk shadows zebra the dirt. Within planes of blue umber, then light,
then umber, the blurred twirl of a leaf
winks 20, 30 yards, descending. A scintilla. An eye,
like the others. Autumn opens as radiance, closes
as stone. Under a pressure nobody can imagine
there's a central cubic inch of this planet, a black incandescence
towards which everything falls
yet I've never been, can never be, happier
and no reason—or none weightier than mountain air
leaking gold. Which no sooner seems an "Oktoberfest"
than out of the word's transparent German
a girl's smile comes to me, surviving only as name, Lily Tofler,
luckless, radiant—just as thinking of stone
I step into sunlight
traversing exactly these branches to reach me.

Ultramarine rings off the summits, their scree-slopes.

The eye opens to brilliance like that, animal and happy
it walks in the sun's perfect circles
helping photons pour from their center out of some vast, casual joy
while our share infinitesimal strikes this earth
and keeps going. That I touched them for others
in me, the words on those gates, or passed through them,

wife and sons with me unharmed, reading "Arbeit Macht Frei"
written in iron on eyes closed as stone
back of the black hinges at Dachau
teaches nothing but luck. Moment to moment
light's witnesses dismantle, annihilate, while every particle
illumined survives, eternal
as matter.

Along faults in this creek making gravity its entire career
fire breaks from pebbles that quench and rekindle
darkness in granite, this sparkling
inside the stream.

With high tides and leaf spills flecking gorse clumps
like pollen, I see warehouses of shoeleather
emptied, bales of shorn hair, gold teeth shoveled up
like shelled corn. But this isn't that light—
in which the shadow of a bullet nine millimeters small
entered the shadow of a girl.

It's just that within the outline of each, the sun
burns to a focus on me
for a moment, never happier.

And the ashen lids of Jewish women squint shut,
wombs injected with mixtures, fine sand in quicklime, hardening
to history. It happened. My kinsmen, the Germans.

Further upslope toward the quarry
I tour the afternoon's plumed and luminous festival,
each aspen a sunburst, a shock, a fire curd I pass through
while October's least breath
offers windfalls of spattered translucence.

In a camp only my kinsmen the Germans could've imagined
I never saw Lily Tofler. It's just that her smile
there, became by-word. Talismanic and mine
now, as it was then for others. A style, a daily, impossible courage
making even the officer's name a matter of record. Whose name
was Boger. Who raped her,

then killed her.

Lapping right up to timberline, the highest trees
seem a gray haze of twig, standing wind-stripped, naked,
accomplished.

In light so dustfree, so moteless these spruce cones
150 yards off cluster their bough tip, glittering
an absolute clarity
what would I know about suffering?
It's just that out of that firebrick and soot centered camp,
through this blind rightness of trees
yellow-breasted as meadowlarks, the name of a girl
comes to me.

Within an amber dazzle of aspen, the sun's circle
half eclipses, trembles—then flares. The eye opens
and closes. And creekwater flashes, leaping down off the peaks,
making up new lives as it runs.

At Luxor

At Luxor we watch an age re-name the profundum
in the name of whatever the sun seemed to be building
in them, or building up to, or towards. Things topple, get squashed.
Turning to look we see eras of folk with both feet mired
in twilight's heavy traffic. We envy their muscular postures
of decaying blur, their appointed times,
and eating the gods like candy—the way puddles on a dirt road
might worship five or six clouds
equally ephemeral.

As if our first mistake on inheriting the mansion
had been detecting gas leaks via lit match
we stepped into their sunlight
only to find its fires planning a second career
as blown star.

Yet the sun's works and days
still leave beautiful stains in the sky, mornings and evenings.

At Luxor we walk around absorbed
by leagues of blood rock whose steep, light-bitten walls
a sundial's one tooth has chawed into rags.
Under them, out of the burnt colors of sandstone,
this pharaoh and his queen gaze far over the valley
like a strange pair of hands in the house next door
playing an absconded piano.

25

The Fifth Season

Up a ladder weightless as bird legs, thinner
than the indelible grass
where thistle leafs out, sizzling like bacon fat,
I'm re-ascending to heaven, getting back into management.

In no time I've persuaded underweight creeks to invest themselves
in the Green, the Yampa, the San Juan, the Gunnison
as they go bandsawing deeper into their canyons
or meander flats, watering acorns programmed
with daydreams and applause for shorelining reservoirs.

I feed a magpie on seeds wanting to fly.
I remind burrowing prairie dogs to exchange and dissolve
into offspring. I nudge cottonwood lint across the Divide
while its tree stays behind
riffling, lacing the San Luis Valley with plankton.
I stock the sky's night waters with dim barge-loads of turquoise
before lofting them southerly, just under the moon.

Off seasons? There are none.

I go round stuffing fresh meadows under old snow,
arrange high-country silences so comprehensive
that only in them can each smallest cony or pine finch
or pipit
take its place and be heard.

I make certain no note is lost. I traffic in light
the eye has not seen.

Out of stumps and trunks and fallen limbs moldered,
out of the white-bellied slugs, out of silver leaves
trilling sage stalks; out of bindweed
scribbling its inexhaustible phrases, the sulphur-flowers
yellowing wind, the daytime galaxies thicker than powder,

quicker than number; out of pollen scum
dusting pools in the rock,
out of the four suns of Colorado's four seasons
I send a fifth season up in its skies, rising always.

Is my ladder still there? One rung at a time
I begin to step out of heaven, a cloud's possibilities
descending, as if some pure volunteer—or common starling
dead in mid-flight,
flashing dark color off preen oil
in wings barely stirring, whispering
ever so lightly as its slow turn falls
perfectly aimed
through air's open doors
toward the exuberant wreckage of August.

TWO

Essay on Air

The air is a nest of gears that mesh,
those floral repeats lapping your dining-room wallpaper,
before the house was pulled down.
The air ticks.
It is air you must lean on to see
that the island below in the Loire
is actually a woman in bed with a snake.
Elsewhere, Ceylon, labyrinthine atmosphere
wandering the green floor of a field involves
a particular lizard: noosed in a blade of grass.
As for"air tragedies," a modest prominence
in Central Turkey is the current record holder,
300 in one collage. The air of July
teaches us how to chisel lace doilies
of ice, whereas January air blowing off the moon
sets our lungs to scuba diving amongst reefs
of blue fishbones that feign *les neiges d'antan*
otherwise the unspeakable air of summer.
That ladder of wingprints your soul
is the air of a non-Euclidean gnat
wintering off India's southeastern coast.
The air hermetically sealed in Bosch's triptych
turns little red berries into the bait of lust.
It is the varnished air of the Pinakothek
that sends us out into the Ringstrasse to find them.
Air's effects are timed:
The autumnal air of driveways; inciting
dried points on mortgaged oak leaves to pretend
they inscribe suitable sentiments in concrete
as they crab along, already late
for your appointment.
From snapshots, the catch-and-ratchet air
of sodium hypothiosulfate can tighten
that old violin wire your heart,
where two friends, forgotten all these years,

31

turn aside from the lake. The air of a woman's bra
missing from the doorknob can close
that distance between nostrils and thought
like a hand inside a thigh
as the body hair of her voice
selects appropriate fuse lengths:
the venous system, the arterial system.
Indeed, the bloodstream of air is a machinery
meshing interchangeable parts.
Respiration: our word that has swallowed
the circumnavigation of air. In it you sense
gearprints tiny as clawtips on four
small feet, and a tail, that have for years
been winding your breath
into the sound of this page, this moment, this room
where for all we know, to fill out the last gasp
of even a lizard dying across the way
in Ceylon, the air might have begun
here and now; is beginning, in fact,
at your little finger.

Jane,

Like a hand waving home from a postcard
a single cloud drifts summer's last word
over the lake. And a Steller's jay flashes past
skimming shoreline, tracing its serial of well-managed falls
on wingfeathers blue as a kitchen match, tossed
—then quenched among pine boughs.

How many and wordless the miracles, how few
our little flicks of amazement.

Could we have guessed a year ago, here,
Bear Lake's doubled trees, doubled cliffs,
islanded boulders would fuse
once and for all
to that instant I saw you were dying?

My eyes, yours—their green irises sunlit
and brilliant—suddenly seeing into each other
across the one impossible distance.

Alone, walking the rich carbon muck
edging a tarn, I look back every so often
for no reason, the only reason,
watching how one after another, and slowly,
the late afternoon's brimming ultramarine
seeps into bootprints.

Reflections of air
filling all but my most recent steps
with its clear, material silence.

Poem

Less and less steeped in the sun's vegetable dyes
autumn's synapses harden to the boneyard colors
of ditch weed going reedy and thick.

In upper levels of sky
the wind sees more and more of its breath.

And one morning, a white midnight sleeps over
waking frozen to twigs, fog's motionless reef
whose branches blacken again by mid-afternoon.

But by then the sun's a red diver.

Snowfields blur and hurry.
A fence post's long shadow falls flat in the road
and dissolves, sifted away, like these questions
we keep setting aside
as if our best bet lies in not asking.

"How many eons till spring?"

Don't we hope scanning for moonrise
out over the prairie teaches zero is nothing?

Just a moment that falters, the heart
sensing each beat of its way.
Up from locked ploughlines, one cold
and violent bubble of stone mechanically rises
wrapped in our own dumb flame.

Skiing Alone Near the Divide

1.

The sun's a ghost chicken, haggard smolder, a flare
and dissolve into snowfall where nobody's been
but more weather.

It pours down that continuous fault we call the Divide
yet you love driven crystal
faintly sizzling your windbreaker, love
the shut whisper of skis over snowpack
so cold your pole-tips croak
like white frogs.

2.

Even air this thin has its animals.

A chittering flock of them, birds
tiny as seedpods throated with rust,
hustles the black asterisk pine-tops, veering,
pecking terrain so starved its pain seems yours—
moving, inhuman—so long ago you remember
more dimly than sunset at 4:21
putting Jasper Lake well beyond daylight.

3.

Like mountain-maple's twig sheaves, exposed,
snatched naked, like gorse dwarf, fir paralytics
gnarled leeward, your compass is wind
incessant and westerly
as your fascination with going too far,
into that breath where the body ends
and willpower takes over.

The lake out of range. Finding you haven't the energy
you find that's where you're aiming.

4.

To turn off wind you ski into timber
like closing vault doors on a radio,

entering cloud shelved high among boughs loaded,
overloaded with powder quietly adding flake
upon flake. Quietly, the way sweat ices up

fleecing color from mittens, headband and nape,
eyebrows, wool knickers.

5.

Under the heaviest limbs
of the year's darkest trees this forest floor
is meteors of snow
settling differences—between warring outcrops, snags,
smashed ledges, zapped logs that took flight
headlong into ravines.

Their casual slaughters, resolved. One undulant dune
of visible stillness.

Is this what a truce
might suddenly sound like? You listen for flaws.

All you can hear is your own breathing.

The Fire Thief

Blood moon, my face. Hovering fire
that centers our house like a great, warm-bosomed taproot
herding its tree through the frostbitten stars
of dead winter. Abed, my father knows nothing.

The iron door ajar, I stand at a forge, a caldera,
draw forth our poker, heat-ripened, a brand, a red sceptre, a power
more outrageous than any abuse I could think of.
Who'd have supposed our whole house was in motion?

Against its heaviest footfall, I recharge that poker,
take aim at one wicked head, then douse its luminous rage
in old ashes where it fumes, smoldering—
half heat, half dust—while I clean up the basement.

At the bottom of winter's an iron door ajar,
and a father who doesn't dream, has no way of knowing
I return there every so often, just to stand in that season
where every household burnt coal, poking embers

that stir as if an old meteor could slow to a puddle, revive
for a while, and beat like some fat, animal heart
once familiar. Then dim, ashing over
till it seems to know nothing of motion,

coming in second to snowflakes.

North

Its night is this three-quarter moon
made of snow. A continent is born, or an otter. And dies.

Tamarack limbs near the clearing sag with snow.
The tarns are blind with it. The whole valley is luminous.
Clear as a rifle
lake-ice splits, scattering echoes.
The wolf halts. Her snout comes up. Her ears
flick and stand. The cedars creak, taking great cold
into their bodies.

She looks into her world like a thing that is there.

She is not afraid to see where it goes. She listens,
leans forward. In a sky like one wide constellation
stars made of nothing but fire and ice
put the moon on her breath.

THREE

Vespers

In my ear the evening hush rustles
like grasshopper bones—and Augustine speaks to me
of the "fair harmony of time."

Over the broken Divide, western clouds slog along
like tired festival workers in a winepress, stunned
on color. Everywhere, the Hieronymus Bosch country.

"Your bones snow into the earth,
isn't that both sides of the question?"

And now the dark begins to develop
further back than the pyramids, hyper-considerably.
One by one its infinities gleam, printing the blood
between my every two pulses. This thick stellar traffic
my past always shoots me among—where the simplest words
like "In the beginning . . ." explode.

Dream shrapnel, the brain—its light at this hour
always frantic with meditations on some One
as the grenade of its choice not to exist
for billions of years, if ever. Out there
burning incomparable tracks.

"How do you take your daisies?"
"Oh, radiant, I guess. Through the eyeballs
like nails. Like this."

Stopping for Lunch I Take Off My Skis and Sink Up to My Pockets

I.

Like wide drops of dark oil
the wren's eyes glisten South Seas
descending as snow all afternoon. It flitters twig
a ski-length away, as if I'd never killed birds.

Merely unwrapping a sandwich barehanded
thickens blood to almost a standstill.
Re-mittened, the fingers return loaded with pain
as if stepped on by hammers.

Wind nudges spruce tops. Over legs thin as grassblades
the wren's tailfeathers cock like a tic, lower slowly, re-cock.
A heart that must equal the heft of a leafbud,
red-chambered.

II.

How in any such cold so tiny a bird stays alive
I do not know. Just verve too animal to clear out
and leave polar weather.

Just eyeless design
risen from mud into its bloodstream
and mine. An aim that wants to keep moving and warm
after every limb, every stone in this forest has crumbled.

The wren flicks, keeping an eye on me
sidelong. Overhead, the snow pinnacles lift dazed faces
empty as fact. Yet even they may know something,
if less than a nail remembers of ore. Some one dull thing
infra-dim, pitifully. Dim beyond measure.
Less than ashes remember of fire.

III.

Anaxagoras guessed the primal atom held every bootprint
I make, saw the least of these iced pinecones
already there, within it, imagined. Even my mitten
touching the space left by a whir
flown headlong into evergreen glooms—on wingwork impossible
and easy as never having been here at all.

And all the while asking, "What was it our comings and goings
made part of?"

The white cliff near one summit
stares into cloud as if stranded with us
in time. Bewildered, forlorn. Like some strange desolation
that meant to look on, groping up and down
in the blood till someone, stopping here,
comes to the memory we wanted.

West

100 meters more
thwacking your left boot, right boot
into blue windpack, then 50, then the summit.

Widespread as cloud, the snow peaks burn.

They brighten each eye
as you stand facing nothing
but the mirage of the real
between you and all the strange places
you came from.

Sundown and red wind.

Your hair has caught fire.
Your skull is a comet.

In the Iron Trough of the Year

At night stepping out to drive the car
into the garage because it may snow,
or retrieve a pop-bottle tossed onto dead grass
we notice how the usual innumerable stars
annually freshen and seem to draw near
the nearer we draw to Christmas.

"Once upon a time" was then. So we're stuck
like these elms and 2 peartrees, half dead,
our kids bored with the sky. No ermined riders on camelback
straggling down from the edges of dunes,
nor blue-knuckled hicks
warming themselves at a pinch of radiance
tufted in straw. In the iron trough
of the year, all there is
is ourselves, and whatever we offer
is not what anyone wanted, or how.

And if the southern horizon features a planet
so dazzling its glint rinses the eye, we're sure
it can't have been *that* one,
though almost equally luminous—

Or so we suppose, even if good for nothing we know
except to bear witness: that we swim in a dark
full of fireballs, of centaurs and harps
and lions diagrammed, and the bright stance
of old-fashioned gods in their odd, posthumous
flourishings. The nightly mysterious scene
as it is now. As its mystery has ever been
and may be, world without end; and yet
perhaps not entirely beyond us.

Eyes that Opened Me

Between the sky in the mind,
the mind in the sky, this lifetime of shoeleather.

And a few whispers.

Ones that were hers
at the tip of the ear, melting
the North Pole's invincible nail.

And her look, coming with me, more entirely
than any moment I remember, actually us
open eyed
where no promise
remained to be spoken or kept
in this world, or forgiven
in all its promising emptiness.

Rimlight and Pupil

Think how much of this gorge you keep mistaking
for praise, skiing uphill on creek beds loaded with powder
sown hour after hour, steady as clock ticks
floating down windless.

Consider how remotely this afternoon sky offers its blue
beyond reason, a blue ringing in the eye like iron
while local disasters blaze smoking away
off the summits. And how their backlit chimneys of snow
whirlwind and prism, rainbowing in pure illustration
these colors we see by are blind, which is why
we must praise them
and why our amazement means nothing.

Trail your way up the last bouldered snowfield
given to cliff and look into faces
profoundly empty as praise,
all summer lakes frozen. And sense how late afternoon chill
deepens skiing alone, where all you lay eyes on
ignores what it means to be human.

As small bodies of cloud drift into the sun
tearing themselves slow limb from limb in sheer incandescences
that arrest you, examine by what least shift in your stance
a solar ray flaring off this ingot of ice
is eclipsed by rock shelf overhead. Feel what a long moment
your pupil moves into out of that fire
and how long you mean to remember.

And how long you mean to remember its haloes
of freeze coating quartz nodules, cinder inclusions,
icicled snags of uprooted juniper, till the whole burning rim
kindles your awe
that such an immense desolation
is no truer than we are. And that we will not die.
And that nothing can save us.

FOUR

The Blue Changes

To read the blue changes
spot the cony that chitters, the rock top
where a second cony replies.

Notice how the tiny necks stretch forward
emitting birdcalls from fur,
chirrups and tweets that beat time, drifting into sync
then out, like turn signals at an intersection.

Allow snowfields to float on illusions of haze
so unrifted you can't find the least foundation
their summits might rest on. While shadows of cloud
slide up and down, dappling white mountains, translate
their blue changes written on snow
to a fable in which the lightest gesture is ageless
and nothing repeats.

Compare the deep immobilities of these ridgelines
with themselves
happened in an eyeblink
and inhale the peace of tremendous devastation
light-years slower than yours.

Despite the brain's "Forget it, nobody's there"
examine your vision, hungering after the profiles of others,
instilling this or that granite fleck with a stance
remotely companionable, miming dark rock
after dark rock alive
because your eye won't believe what you tell it.

Trick the 2 downhill swallows blurting through flurries
of snow into animating this entire gorge
as if the only ones here.

Looking closer, insist on that outline

within range of your voice
till the eye gives in. A shape toppled from stone
face down in spring powder. While the mind wavers
wondering if only your name
can reach him, measure the size of its quiet
as pinpoint. Listen to the six-sided ice
ticking the hood of your parka.

Equinox

That nick on the scale
where day and night weigh the same. Green ensilage
of foothills, Colorado mesas
weedy enough to scythe. And past the bikers, the joggers
this car drives up in front of our neighborhood
covered with snow.

Or a black Cadillac passes the doorsill
where two Savannah women are smoking
little twisty cigars. For as long as the cortege
takes to go by the elderly peanut vendor stares
holding his baseball cap in his hand
weighing its flowers.

Anne, Your Name's Mouth and Kiss

How many seasons has the almanac stuttered
and threatened granite's iron slam
its guillotine yawn? Striking dumb all wood sorrel
hollyhock, all low-as-crocus
or sand-lily sounds
overheard within the hum of your name.

Who'd dream of a slab for his pillow? Who would?
No man, no matter how meanwhile
and starved and incessant the black ice encroaches
proffering withered selections
cube-rooted in zero

—far from your syllable's
chère reservoir, its *primavera* and daybreaks
over clear water

without whose reflections for pollen, for sepal
I'd be Januaried eons of dubious moons, all apple boughs
skeletal
utterly birdlorn and skeletal

until
or unless

your name's mouth and kiss
its branch and clean flowering
spoken
gives tongue to the year
as if seashell
and my stalled skies widen their circles

like one simple blossom's arrival
reviving
deep in the eye
light's body.

Why I Marvel at Certain Noises

Isn't it a world where mothers give birth
to snowmen who waking discover they're us
becoming again the text of the dream?

And after hiking all afternoon don't the eyes
trek home as if from a banquet, stuffed
with ephemeral landscape?—and with studying herds

of deer, watching them nibble at meadow-browze
while guessing which is Nebuchadnezzar. Returning
to our own kind, don't we pore over faces

like those who'd believe in sortilege? As we dwindle
to an indefinite few remaining words, doesn't our gaze
weave through air-terminal crowds as if to retrieve

from nobody we know the look of a lost life
stepping towards us? My marvel is therefore
at such riddling terms as "alone"; at enigmas

pronouncing like "stranger." And in an atmosphere
shared, can't tiny historians threading every ear
from mine to listeners long before the flood

suddenly blurt down or into and out of
these cloudy dust-greens on our Russian olive
wearing just sparrows for gloves?

Tiber

Near the Castello Sant'Angelo you pause on the bridge
letting all traffic sounds flow.

Out of the sun's razzle on water
helmets come to you, shattered ones, fire-new from the anvils,
rivited bucklers, corselets magnificent, magnificent dintings
in five-folded shields with Etruscans
thrown down their own wells, with Volces
slaughtered while fording the river
and with all the hacked Oscans and Samnites.

Each travertine pier on the bridge
keeps ploughing upstream, upstream, upstream.
The Tiber flows down. The traffic goes nowhere.

And in tridents abandoned, they rattle, the atoms.
Their invincible valences rattle.

Prospectus

No men, no women?

None. A handful of pronghorn browse
and doze. Wind freshens, gusting creosote
nobody owns or regards. Dawn imagines cliff-faults
grey and second-hand as old shacks
cleansing themselves,
turning rose by degrees.

Yet certain turbulences survive?

The hurt coyote with folded forepaw; wingspan,
shading fast over stubble whose fieldmouse
freezes; magpie colonized by red ants.

Is weather peculiar; anything like that?

A veritable wind—no longer
that ventriloquist's dummy—released now
for tirelessly loving its work: magnificent storms,
torrential thunders hammered of lightning
and rains meaning nothing.
Across former faces of ploughland, the sable,
the white, the viridian seasons swallow each other
the way cumulus scuds or goes to pieces
or drifts, lacking
even ghosts of ideas.

But isn't this light the identical day's end
where all of us used to stand?

Yes. Nothing's changed. Streams,
ponds, still held in place by that same
blue and darkening slab of air.
Of course none of the sunsets

are ports; the evenings neither empty
nor full. Incomparably so.
Full and untroubled forever.

As for nights—how is it they manage?

Without a single tongue
to form "moon," a creamy, voluble thing
rides freely relieved of its name.
None to follow, below, thinking "luminous
tomb lid"; simply a husk, an empty boat
whose brightness quietly rows
through cloud, dragging the lake
for our shadows.

FIVE

Out of the Ashes of Last Summer's Green Cigar

Speaking of what's touched, not held,
forget how this extravagant pebble falls
between steps, how the sun
splashes up out of mud, blossoms, flops back in ruins
whose tunnels we stare into and never return. Limbs
that hung by the neck until dead
through that long sunset of winter
begin bucking wind like a traveling host,
a revolution with banners.

Gust upon gust thuds into forested pine
swatched along Shannon Hill, smoking with pollen, clouds
streaming torn puffs of yellow a half-hundred yards
still shaped like their trees, ghost evergreen
carrying paleozoic secrets
the first pinecones keep sending forward.

And the spring fields.

Wet, weedy breath taken in from their future, nearing,
fills with the hopelessly promising—ourselves
for once, and this western plateau
and all creatures on it, because any day
out of the burlap smell of spring rains and damp boots
out of the week long winds drying these fields
out of the ashes of last summer's green cigar
a single black cricket
will kindle and kick up its heels
at the end of the world
reconsidered.

Ed & Me

Like twinned mulberry trunks, boys incline
unequally. Out past the C. B. & Q.'s cinder embankment
those green breaks in Mauvaisterre Creek seemed Bengal
on film. Did I say "Bird Island"? Ed favored "Death"
over "Bird," overdoing as always
across his inborn distance, intimate edge.

The hobo lean-to wore sheetmetal tattoos
enameled "Pfister Hybrid for Yield," "Green Diamond Coal,"
"Bear Alignment," with an air hostile
and tribal. Ed was dark, chesty, heroic
to my Gunga Din, all blond sissy-and-bones.
Once after firing up White Owls, Ed took a dump
wiping on burdock, and in we stuck our cigars, burning tips
upright, and stared down the streets of Calcutta.

Through sunflower husk our blue barrels
wavered, steadied to beads. Cardinals we spared
less for plumage than $20 Ed swore
protected Illinois' state bird. Or some code.
Or that redbirds were fastest. When at 32 Ed's liver
"exploded" as Bill Yording put it, from favoring hepatitis
with whiskey, my regrets never reached his survivors,
unsent, unwritten till now,
till even now I'm unsure.

"Blood brothers" I harp on, out of movies, testing
while pulling off sparrow heads
common as popping your knuckles, letting beads
of down-clotted blood deepen our fingers.
Friends incline and forget unequally
then equally. From Ed forever and before first grade
I learned how to lose and be who I wasn't, hard
as character grown to save who we are.

Dark hero, fair sissy. The lost boy
doubles back more and more often the more completely
we've killed him. "Bird Island," where summer survives
beyond recognition, where Ed's name is a glimpse
strange as how I still say it
even saying it now. And a cardinal whirs full speed
into the greenest thicket of hardwoods
as if they weren't there, tossing a single strawberry
to the bottom of India.

Road Life

Why shouldn't you too have a woman?

Because U.S. 36 has always poured possibilities
through your hometown, you squeal smoking out of A&W Root Beer
using acceleration for plumage, letting the road
tell you your story.

Your prospects widen and hum through Missouri
toward Colorado, farm after farm, like a C-Major chord.
At the 7-dollar Peoriana Motel in St. Joe your shower stall
proves roomy enough for even beginners
lathering each other's shoulders and groins. Daylight
for devouring cows in the corn, thunderhead Himalayas; nighttime
for keeping her womb swimming in minnows that fishtail upstream
hundreds of miles, coming along for the ride
through conversation turning on bodies in common
which it turns out you've married. At Marv's Conoco
in Mankato, money-numbers on the gas pump roll up their eyes
and whirl.

While the radio wanders thickets of cowpoke guitar
homegrown in Nebraska, both kids bicker lightly in back
tireless as static playpenned and strapped down for travel.
The prairie goes gusting away, huffing you westerly
down a pipeline of sunsets gaudy as flags
dyed in watermelon slaughter. Sage-clumps whiz by like chenille
fleeing a bedspread. The Jayhawk Rock Shop & Curio Stand
keeps changing name in name only. Near Idalia's town pump
one wind-devil filches salami clear of your sandwich
and feeds it to tumbleweed. Anne laughs
and you laugh and Tim gargles Pepsi.
Nicky skateboards brief swathes of sidewalk at Rest Stops
till wind stuffs you all back into the Chevy.
The game out of Denver is scanning through bug-splat
for the first cloud become mountain.

Overtaking Rainbo Bread your Plymouth kicks ass, roaring,
squeezing ahead of the fumes—
easier, now Tim's helping drive. Unlike yours
his mind doesn't wander. Nick cruises elf wars and gold,
unreeling *Hobbit* cassettes into his ear, dozens of counties.
Then Tim says he's had it, pulling over to put something down
on his own machine. Staggering in the backlash of trailers
you reason irritably before giving in,
watching your firstborn shrink to nearly a man
on his own in the rearview mirror. The way a bird turns tail,
flaps a while, and dissolves.

Cruising past herds of fur money on ranches
you and Anne settle down at 65 miles an hour
to August evenings from the porch, where you drift closer
to each other, to both boys well-married, to the end of the debts.
Because you're a blur making time
like everyone else you've had to re-invent the wheel,
the birthday, the anniversary—their innumerable one or two ways
to turn things, hold things
that never hold still.

You speak to the Day-Glo Vest Committee of the repair crews,
to the flag ladies, to the whoop-and-holler of schoolkids
sucked into vanishing points on your bumper chrome.

You speak to each Stuckeys & Texaco, their marriage of sweetness
and gas. You speak to a chicken hawk veering down slowly
into a nest of blue trees.
You startle at tires suddenly brought to a boil
over bridge floor—and at a fisherman's canvas chair, bright yellow,
left on a sandbar.

You notice Nick noticing how shift-levers handle.

Now that the pavement's half-glaze, now that the family
travels with you by phone, the Volvo feels emptied of traction.
A slipsteam of snow rushes up and over your face.
You lean toward the windshield to sense how your future is doing.

Climbing eastward from Glenwood Springs you follow two eagles
where canyon wall stacks up hundreds of levels
like memoirs housed in a library

including feathered lances and shields,
warpainted bright as a boast
outside Shoshone Hydro Electric. For lunch
why not try the road's shoulder, just short of the Divide
and sentimentalize missing Indians?

With beer and pastrami you enjoy yellow rock
outcropped through snow fallen at the end of winter.
Occasional blazes of sun slur through cloud's lucent moments
while out-of-state plates marvel everywhichway,
enchanted with clifflines. What do the Indians say?
They say flow is their only idea, and that every lost arrow,
every bone in this canyon is happy. Douglas fir brighten,
dim, re-brighten, hovering drifts, illumined
as if roots might emit a light of their own.

Downhill out of the Eisenhower Tunnel
an Impala shoots like sperm
stuffed with young faces and hair, skis on the roof,
the driver a kid who nods, keeping time
to a rhythm he mistakes for his tapedeck
while sucking a blue cocktail stir
and hugging his girl.

How you love them, these touches only the road could imagine!
Because the road still tells a good story
about small figures pretty much like yours
charging the horizon. And tells how, against astonishing odds
often including themselves,
most people get where they're going. Even in the hurtle
and chinook of the vast swashbuckling diesels
you hear it. And, during hushes between,
in these small secrets being traded by birds.

66

Neither Lions Ravens Nor White Toads

It's not ravens. Which of us
can tell them from crows?
Instead, a slip of the wheel, the car
turned safety pin they unlock
with a torch.

It's not the owl's insomnia, boding,
but a golfer at the clinic
looking up from graph-paper to say
"One of your cells has gone mad
and is doubling your bets at 16 feet
per second per second."

It's not any lion crawling forth
from a stone, nor a white toad,
nor pomegranate
with a single lethal seed
but someone bored emptying drawers
into cartons, wondering why
we kept even half.

A wife whose mirror adjusts.
Children who are otherwise occupied.

And dawn stepping out of the elevator
cheerfully, punctually
as if nothing were missing.

When My Name's a Camper's Spoon

Oddest of fears—that the inevitable
might happen. Or that north enough
won't always be south.

When my name's a camper's spoon found among leaves
not even a word in strange mouths
won't there come a warm, a round blue wind
finally coughing up snow
where a timberline butters itself with greens
and Andromedas of cinquefoil cups?
And about that time
won't jaybirds thwack down
into thimbleberry wands ripping open?
And won't they unpack clumsy reed flutes?
And traveling past bristlecone's oldest warps
under the sun on this earth
once I've hiked entirely into my love of these things
won't you still hear
from those ice jaws of couloirs, trickles
slipping loose to be creeks? And hear
whose creekwaters they join, setting out yet again
from the end of the story? Setting out
once more to be summer.

SIX

Remember Black Lake in Winter?

How the granite scarps circled,
rose up, and opened, taking you in—
one steep caldera of ice
not easy to ski toward.

Flashing down now at the outlet,
waters from the end of that world.

Reflections that freshen the sky.

To think that at timberline
fathoms deep under snow, this green
final tree kept insisting. Even here
it can be done.

The Blue Wall of Summer

The blue wall of summer,
colors of evening
and distance. The gold wall, colors of stone
like burnt clay, and fireweed, and bread.

Ron, the one thing Ouzel Lake
knows how to do at this hour
of dusk ripples—is barely to breathe.
Is to rest under an animal film,
a living membrane
with twilight in its keeping.

Not a cloud in motion, the dark trees
saying nothing at all. How many miles
carrying great weight have we come
just to listen?

Cigar

Setting fire to the nightly cigar
you hear a kid shaking watermelon seeds in a paper bag
like moths rattling lampshade
as if wrapping the bulb with string.
Why is he turning his back?

In the burnt air of a 30¢ Garcia y Vega
you study carbon copies of your last breath
which turns out tonight
to be blue, and reflective. Smoke's lavish curves
outline strains in the ambiance, drifting unchanged
through windowscreen.

The bulb is night baseball and bugs. Kenny Suttles pumps,
kicks, lets fly. In center, your quadriceps
cock with each pitch
where you prowl chiggery mats of rust clover
collecting line drives in catches so surprising
they've outlived your gloves and your speed.
Since when have you gone in for cigars?

And when was it he first refused to come with you?
Or the brunette—the one whose eyes and smile
would've saved your life. The woman
you never met, only married. The woman
who ruined it?

Up the chrome ladder she streams from the pool
laughing, straddling your legs with hers
letting poolwater prism and spatter so clearly
you see how it works, total summer
distilled to a droplet. To this one
she's letting him catch on your tongue.

73

The Sleeping Porch

An early meadowlark calls like a hinge lacking oil
and from the sleeping porch that fades
as air-conditioning takes over
I hear a dipper lip clink against pump iron
while Uncle Paul fills then rinses, as always,
three times. Then hear him swallowing . . .
swallowing. . . .

Down Yucca Drive somebody's Toyota won't catch,
chicken squawk scatters, flocks back,
percolates
till Grandad Rexroat's a whiff, grainsacking
sold off with the harness-shed floorboards
the windmill and troughs, the busheled potatoes
his root cellar wears on its breath. Or a hot wind
flows all morning long off the mesa
snapping my neightbor's flag to attention
again, again, till I'm four
under June maples still on that corner, a thought
darker than now; Grandmother Saner is reading the flag
to me, color by color, like gospel.

Her phrase, "your last drop of blood" sticks
to a muzzy shot
featuring Uncle Clarence's lawnmower haircut,
that packet of letters his tidy white cross
in Lorraine keeps mailing
into the attic, all the way from World War I.

Out in the drive
slowing tires crunch brushed aggregate
to a standstill. A car door latches open, clacks shut
on footfalls a father traces into my ear
disappearing over red shale.

Windowscreened splashings. Our sprinkler left on?
Entire lives turn in their sleep, waking
into mine easily as dawn's steady leverage of rust
translates Uncle Paul pumping cistern water.

The way one little twist
of baling wire looped through its cup-handle
can center whole families. Or a knuckle
scuffed against oakgrain
re-builds the barn.

Wearing Breakfast for Two

In that Norway maple outside
a bluejay believing it's somebody's soul
tears seed from the feeder. An elderly couple
pass by under our bedroom window, so subliminally
I peek over the sill only to find their skin
already greatly evaporated. Even a glance
shows that inside his wristwatch
it's distantly raining.

Then you turn up at the bedside
wearing your tastiest smile, as if breakfast for two
and get in.

"So this is the river again, comrade."

We stroke slowly at first, taking it easy,
strong swimmers just warming, up pacing each other.
"Or look at it this way," I start to explain, "that fuse
your body is lighting . . ." And then
our tandem grenade.

Chores face us square in the eye
and places to get to—our Saturday routines
of habitual usefulness—but for the nonce
we must lie very still, listening
to nowhere at all, or to a bluejay, or a cottonwood tree
that thinks it's a river
till pieces enough of ourselves
wash up on the opposite shore.

Stars, and Orion the Hunter

The night, black with attractions.

My hands are being watched,
your lips are under surveillance.
Each star, prying into all of our secrets at once
while knowing nothing about us.

We say, "How thickly sown
the nights ahead are going to be!"

No answer. "If only you knew
how much we wanted to live among you!"

Just brilliance, mere brilliance.

As if fire, every trace of our lives burnt away,
came to light without hesitation
we watch Orion the Hunter—winding in all the sleepers
living and dead. Taking us prisoner, confusing
your name with mine, tying our hands

face to face with each other.

Anasazi, the First Coloradans

They knew next to nothing about the sky
while counting on it for everything.

What a wonderful time that must've been—
to see the sun down, not a twilight clue
where it goes as it vanishes
or why.

And then they cleared out,
leaving behind lots of strange names
and all this furniture.

The Day Wilderness Moves into the Dictionaries

Like a blind man staring into black water, they'll lean
out of all sight, the tottered, ramshackle hemlocks.

Among a cirque's mess of echoes
nobody is going to hear, a jet's engines will dissolve
with their vapor trails high over cloud
covering tarn bottoms veloured with algae, over creeks
teeming minnowed char, semi-transparent.
After three days of on and off rain
the lower summits will begin emerging like elders
who find they've nodded off for a moment. Slow as the moon
low veins of mist will warp and hover
forested valley.

Where some 15 or 16 head of blue caribou
are grazing tilted horizon
their lips curl back, their teeth tear at the grasses
in a stillness with the texture of dream.

Near boulders
like a language beheaded
the lead animal browses tussocks. His antlers
waggle almost to his hooves as he munches,
moves forward. Stepping delicately
where no one can, ever.

SEVEN

Ghiberti's Baptistery Doors Revisited

What flawless boredom, the Renaissance. Adam dreams
as advertised. Patriarchal though muddied the Father
draws from him a woman rising impeccably
as palmfrond incised beyond date-trees. Like stories
that walk in our sleep, Abraham's blade stresses
Isaac's bared throat. Though today's gesture of pipe
and fulminate exploded the bombmaker's lap,
in this antiqued sky relieved by wings
and under the Duomo's red tile balloon floating
a tombstone, the angel's hand stays him.
Yet these are the doors.

Joshua, aging, boards my No. 25 bus on partisan feet
left half snowbanked near Appenine pass. This *virtù*
in Jacob's thigh volubly turning, striking his bargain
for a Rachael cherishable as our illusions of becoming
I could reach to and touch, touch the burnish
on Lot's nose, Solomon's wisdom and fingers
while Aldo Moro feels the first 1 or 2
of 11 slugs produce his corpse for TV. Reachable
with a single paving block hurled, Benjamin
stands surrounded for sale by brothers. Italy, as ever,
gang war. And still these are the doors.

Immortal tons of ennui. Because Ghiberti fell
between sculptor, jeweler? Or because Rebecca's sisters,
16 and 7, got molotoved last night by mistake? The giltwork
blisters, leaking bronze through gold fog
like rust on heaven's gates. And Adam yet dreaming.
Millennially, I suppose. Dreaming Eve before Abel
and Cain, Esau denied, David hounded by Saul.
Of Eve who rises up entirely, here
where these are the doors.

Song for Sisyphus

Evenings, Sisyphus watches the stone
get away, bounding downhill, cartwheeling,
buzzsawing through yucca—a lichened meteor overland
till wobbled asleep at the foot of the mesa.

Spent motion he refuses to take for an answer.
Or any motion ending in heaviness.

Mornings, while the easterly edges of earth
come up with bright ideas
like a fresh approach to the problem, again he sets forth
heartened by promises, unforgettable ones

of dusted vapor. And color. And air.

Late Roman Mosaic: Husband and Wife

From our glass dazzle, our nacreous inlays, aureoles
rimmed in purples, arterial reds,
we regard you with eyes balanced exactly
as goldsmith's balances weighing air,
weighing you as you are, less now
than a moment ago.

What might we say? That the river sleeps
in the cloud, then falls, breathing
fresh ruin into the shoots of myosotis?

Yes. And that we have turned to look, turned
at the burning membrane of yet another world
whose sky is a wish, the story
of a continuous heart re-telling itself in you
our own shadows, trembling.

Who Knows Better than These?

It comes to us out of the blue in Ravenna
not a soul knows who we are
better than these blessed saints eyeing us freshly
as bottle-glass shattered. Closer, we're woven agate,
flint bits, nibs of Alsatian jasper, vitreous paste,
chalcedony—puzzled fabric for St. Damian's robe,
as if stepped from the flashiest veins
of a coal miner's daydreams.

Through sacred broadsides of shale once entire, stone robins
fly up from the bowels of geology
to sprint ozone's late-Roman
over a St. John so eager and frank
his Revelations seem lip-synched with red shift
and a planet in atoms.

How still and frontal and simple.
Drifting basilica naves here in Ravenna
we're nebular fires glued to the walls like windshields
crazed at high speeds,
assemblies of saints looking through them
prophetically, each blessed facial grenade
promising everything back to the sky.

What Do the Aspen Say?

We open, we breathe. A lithe joy
even in rain, measuring the source of each stream.
Light burns in our leaves, which fall
making way for new buds. And winter sustains them.

We find a flag for each of four seasons. And yours?

Don't you stand on the animal soil
announcing the end of the world is a ridgeline away
as the crow flies?—
turning this world's furthest travels to stone.

Centering each brain, you insist,
is a worm. Your own eye you call a contraption
in love with a star.

We flourish on roots drawn out of the clouds.

In any moment you spend dissecting
just one of our branches
they'll have flown with us for thousands of miles
yet only through you
could we have heard that their fire
is accidental, and borrowed.

We open, we breathe
an affluent and limber joy. Like all living things
we are the worse for man. What light
do you sow here? You mumble, you mutter and stare.
You believe in dark knowledge.

Green Feathers

Five minutes till dawn
and a moist breath of pine resin comes to me
as from across a lake. It smells of wet lumber, naked and fragrant,
whose sap is another nostalgia.

In the early air
we keep trying to catch sight of something lost up ahead,
a moment when the light seems to have seen us
exactly as we wish we were.

Like a heap of green feathers poised on the rim of a cliff?
Like a sure thing that hasn't quite happened?
Like a marvelous idea that won't work?

Routinely amazing—
how moss tufts, half mud, keep supposing
almost nothing is hopeless. How even the dimmest potato
grew eyes on faith the light would be there
and it was.

Waking to the Ceiling of an Italian Farmhouse

My look blurs on Anne's hair
swimming the pillow, clears at the edges, wanders skinned logs
used as roof traves that've been lifetimes of daylight and rain
and will be again.

Lovers met there, when this ceiling was groves?
Most likely. How ancient, the shelf-life
of cypress. "Gian Angelo ... Gian Angelo?" she calls
from Wars of the Spanish Succession. And he,
barely audible, "Rosanna? ..."

Body and words. Elysian winds. The inner ear
is made of them.

Yet I'm glad my bloodstream's part of that letter
the dead keep sending themselves,
that one where Chaldeans, Alamanni, Samnites and Visigoths
danced at our wedding, making us gifts
of our children.

Gino's footsteps on gravel. Our rooster crows
like rust on a lop-sided axle, or that gate-creak
of the chickenyard as Gino side-steps
into hen ruckus, rattling his pail, strewing cracked grain.

Mixed with spatters of chaffinch.

Even through this green morning gloom
of closed shutters, I feel the dead setting out their marvels
offhandedly. Scents of wisteria, lemon tree. Wrens
by the shoal. And tanagers. A great-grandmother's youth
shining in Anne's mussed hair.

How casually we drop off
toward the deepest part of that family

whose voices no one can hear. Then wake
as a daïly, nameless desire flutters open the eyelids
where each of their mornings takes root.

If You've a Leaning Toward Pillars of Fire

I.

Once when the only talk was heat
these rocks were a mist. Now summer daylight
burns the range's snowpack like candles.

Beyond that line where trees grow to fit the wind
a bush writes brief stories
reading like the slower weather
of schist. Indian flowers prance red, yellow
blue—thumb-high and prodigal,
blossoming elements
torn loose by the roots, under skylines
waving their bones, under peaks like gravity's canon.

And we travel altitude's sheer thornbush of granite
till the next step is air.

Looking down
into gullies choked with stone zoos
stampeded from slopes, we remember passing into
and through another life to get here, the one
where we started, and cliffs offering its relics,
seamarked, 12000 feet up.

II.

Pitched above timberline you can try mixing cigarsmoke
with twilight, while the far plain's
slurred phosphorescences grow to a town
hard to believe we live in.

Or you can follow your elevation as shadow
begun in that plain when slow secrets
cragged like old news

at your back, first unraveled their mineral lightning
under the earth.

If you've a leaning toward pillars of fire
you can look high overhead where sunset's still climbing
—the prodigal towers, the grand rampages of cumulus—
and from the ground up
watch the darkness destroy it.

If you're drawn by distance mixing the purple end
of the spectrum
you can find it—way over there at the edge
though that's what you're touching, the world's rim
with us wherever we stand.

The Vesuvius Variations

I.

Each home has amnesia
about all but a few of its family.

But not how the beanpots stood, what eggshells look like
abandoned. That day the sky fell right here
and doors burnt off their bronze hinges. Where Shelley stood
overhearing oracular thunder. Where a blonde Yugoslav wafts past
catching up to her friends, sandaled and haltered,
touring July in Italy's wall-shadows.

Her breasts bobble, half-running.
The very frescoes act out your yen for her.

At your feet sprawls her copy in chalk, clawing at floortiles,
lips twisted back by sulphur dioxides. Put your mouth to her mouth,
just a touch of your breathing will save her
if only it's Roman.

Because her body is nubile, "caught in the act"
of blind panic, you fall into the stance of morbid detail
her stars might've predicted.

Her mouth's exact convulsion. Isn't its rictus,
gaping, yours at yourself, 2000 years
foreseen? You, the voyeur she gives birth to.

II.

You arrived at Vesuvius by way of the sticks
in downstate Illinois. Cameras, of course. And awe.

And like a gambler cascading marked cards

it still oleanders the brain, *L'Autostrada del Sole*—
median strip in continuous flower all the way here
kilometer after kilometer southward from Rome. The blossoms pour
past your left elbow—every 7th hill antiqued with towns,
azured and dinted ones, housed on terrain merely dormant,
villages fortressed back of pepperstone walls
dim as old women living alone,
wild boars in the basement.

What rustles ahead of you? Women descending
wearing clear plastic bags
over clogs and good loafers. The whole cone's a gala of dust
flicked with polyester dyed bright as fruit rind. Each color a pilgrim
traversing glass ashes. High on the slope their kite-stream
zigzags the footpath—switchback through switchback—
right up to the lip.

That caldera Spartacus chose—to hide rebels, remember?

Smithereened, growing this one. Trash pinnacles, crestfallen walls
far steeper than you'd imagined. Where the ascent
turns promenade, even the eye hesitates,
picks its way down. As if to help you discover
all that you own worth having, new climbers
top out and stroll, or just stand
rimming the edge, gazing in.

III.

Think of the sun as a farmer
brilliantly blind. Of city faces as buds, their tree
leafing out. One soft machine, like any other?—
under volleys of transparent boulders
turning ruddy, darkening as they fall
toward the rooftiles of Julia Felix
still buried.

Fellow flights of crashed eyes. A long stillness . . .
broken by the scrape of a shovel. Then light on your dog, barking
in mosaic . . .

as Leopardi, himself a dark fire, turns aside

nowhere, part of the view. Lava bursts into flower
whose name you pronounce like some talisman, quietly—and again
"*ginestra*"—your breath leaning forward
toward the space left by his.

From Capodichino a jumbo jet
plump as a seedpod
revs, taxis faster, then faster, then rises.

IV.

Blips of Ischian archipelago, possibly Capri, translate the day's heat
into mist intervals, windrows of cloud
under blunt yellow moon.
And you ride at anchor with them, overlooking glitter
so tame all the biremes, skiffs, feluccas,
crews on torpedo boats, seem sunken to rumor.

From the Pensione Stella Maris (*güte küchen*), its patio
scruffy with succulents, African cacti,
you kindle a Swedish timbermatch on terracotta and set fire
to one of your Wild Western cheroots manufactured at Lucca.

Miles away, Vesuvius rides low in the water.

An ortolan flickers lime branches nearby, swishing leaves,
just as gust to gust
this whole island rattles softly. Its laurel, quince,
olive and plum twigs toss through curt elliptical gestures
mechanically, again, again—
as if some portion of air might be of our own design,
which thank goodness it isn't.

You exhale cigar smoke into the hands
of night morning glories trained up on fish twine. You listen.
Little waves, hitting dark rock. Falling to pieces
far as your inner ear's surge and lull—devising,
revising—till any life you can think of seems a tongue
in a tongue in a tongue.

And warps of seabreeze keep slipping ashore,
walking between the geraniums.

95

V.

A merchant sailor comes toward you, stepped from curds
on curds of ginestra, pollen yellow, one cumulus tumble
over the great flow of 1944, turning grit rivers
to scenery.

A sailor who smiles, crossing old fireballs.

If your own smile's a suspicion
too thinly veiled, who hasn't heard the art of Naples is theft?
You light a crooked local cigar at this jet of live steam
they call *fumarole*, offering the sailor a smoke
in your tongue's version of his.

"Keep an eye on your Volvo," he insists, and repeats it. And insists
on showing his papers. The better to con you?

"This world is mud"
said Leopardi, untruly, though true what it cost him,
right up to "La Ginestra" on magma. Isn't that where you are?

With a sailor eager to name ports-of-call: Long Beach
2 months ago, then San Francisco. A sailor afraid
you wouldn't know. Because in America most people work—
but *Napoli*? O Madonna! he sings, Madonna!
all over town
thieves thick as this scrub oak, the very leaves
heavy-lidded watching you dawdle off from your car
to visit the lava.

Where a stranger steps from broom-flower
golden and cockerel, cascading bleak torrents of stone
and crosses to you, and touches—
to save you from thieves, to say, "I've been in your country"—
and no other reason—that too is Naples.

VI.

Watching two swallows above the Phlegraean fields—
high over their bestiaries of ore, slag hogbacks
and immortal dead horses made from stone sun

that wore, once, the slower colors of fire—
you understand
out of the tillage of light
it is flickers only.

It is exactly this sort of sheer
aerobatic roll, veer and swerve
swallows trace mating.

It is only their kind of paired winglash and coupling
and daredevil blurs crossing retinal nerve
with the entire history of swallows
entered into
that can dart, fall, and recover
intricately, ephemerally enough
to sustain us.

VII.

The angelus? From gritty belltowers specked here and there
atop olived ravines, clappers ding, hardly deeper than dinnerbells,
at the twilight rim of your evening.

Air to the second power. And then, and barely, its earliest
half dozen stars.

Vesuvius, half shadow, half glow. Like the red right hand of Jove.

Lounging hotel *terrazza* with bread, cheese, a bottle,
you understand how rumors under the earth
must've deepened these late evening skies, back then,
when the whole thing was gods. Isn't this always the hour
your most radiant germs
would have you believe that cinder and char
riding blue shorelines riding a stone
are not the full story?

From the floor of the forum all the way to your terrace
a puddle of lime poured into an absence, a clot of it,
keeps moving your lips, bearing witness
it was a good life, incomparably so, dying was worth it
and the whole town is happy.

Out of the waxworks, her candle.

"Sit here a while," you say. And she does, drawing breath
tangibly with you, letting her local wine
once again pastel the hilltowns, re-colonizing this shambled
and ravishing bay in deities
gaudy as strato-nimbuses, lavendered.

Their casual artillery waftings
seem to be taking you lightly as a crossroads of moonshine.

A tourist, merely another. Guessing outward from the skin
that your mind may find nowhere to go, may never go anywhere
further than now
where your sense of the air learns how to be ocean,
no shore to its breathing.

As a Fulbright Scholar in Florence, Reg Saner studied Renaissance culture, and has translated works by 20th century French and Italian writers; as a Coloradan of long standing, he has tended to specialize in what men of earlier ages called "the book of nature." He continues an interest in Renaissance cosmology, and is writing an extended critical comment on the poetic image. Saner teaches at the University of Colorado, in Boulder.

His two previous books won awards: *Climbing Into The Roots* (Harper & Row, 1976), the Walt Whitman Award; *So This Is The Map* (Random House, 1981), selected by Derek Walcott in the National Poetry Series Open Competition.